When Betsy came to Babysit

With love for my granddaughter, Summer, who is such a joy to babysit.
E.D.

For my Neeps and the Warings for all your love and support,
and to Patsy and Verna for helping to realize my dreams.
Z.W.

WHEN BETSY CAME TO BABYSIT
TAMARIND BOOKS 978 1 848 53160 4

Published in Great Britain by Tamarind Books,
a division of Random House Children's Publishers UK'
A Random House Group Company

This edition published 2011

1 3 5 7 9 10 8 6 4 2

Text copyright © Elizabeth Dale, 2011
Illustrations copyright © Zoe Waring, 2011
The right of Elizabeth Dale and Zoe Waring to be identified as the author and illustrator of
this work has been asserted in accordance with the Copyright, Designs and Patents Act 1988.

TAMARIND BOOKS
61-63 Uxbridge Road, London, W5 5SA

www.tamarindbooks.co.uk
www.randomhouse.co.uk

Addresses for companies within The Random House Group Limited can be found at:
www.randomhouse.co.uk/offices.htm

THE RANDOM HOUSE GROUP Limited Reg. No. 954009

A CIP catalogue record for this book is available from the British Library.

Printed and bound in China

When Betsy came to Babysit

Elizabeth Dale

Illustrated by Zoe Waring

Tamarind

When Betsy came to babysit
she said to Ria and Josh,
"I don't know anything
    about babysitting!"

"Don't worry!" said Ria. "We will tell you
exactly what we do when we have a babysitter . . .

We always use Mummy's
bubble bath . . .

to wash the cat.

We get out
all our toys and
stay up really, really late.

We go down our slide . . .

and swing
on our swing.

We paint everywhere.

And we make a cake
for Mum and Dad . . .

to show them that
we love them.

We jump on our bouncy castle.

meowwww

We dress up.

Then we make weird noises and scare ourselves silly.

Last of all, we eat ice-cream
and tomato sauce . . .

before we go to sleep on the floor."

"What fun!" said Betsy.
"Now shall I tell you
what I will do?

I will use up all your felt-tips
and colour in all your books.

I will be far too busy eating your chocolates
to read bedtime stories.

Then I will be so full that no one
can sit on my lap for a cuddle."

Ria and Josh looked at Betsy. Betsy looked at them.
"Let's do something new tonight,"
they all said together.

So they did!

The
end

OTHER TAMARIND TITLES:

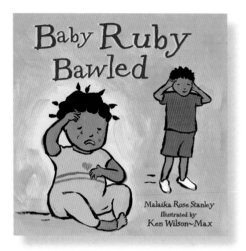

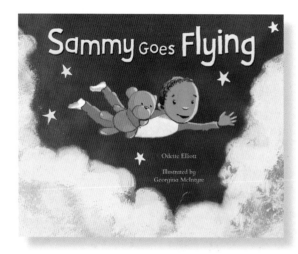

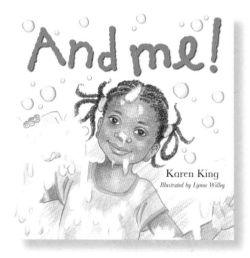

If you'd like to see the rest of our list,
please visit our website:
www.**tamarindbooks**.co.uk